DATE DUE

NOV 02 1994

DEC 23 1995

OCT 31 1996
JUN 28 1997

AUG 18 1998

WITHDRAWN

Niles Public
Library District

6960 Oakton Street
Niles, Illinois 60714
(708) 967-8554

P9-CQF-532

by the same author

MARY POPPINS

MARY POPPINS COMES BACK

MARY POPPINS OPENS THE DOOR

MARY POPPINS IN THE PARK

FRIEND MONKEY

Mary Poppins from A to Z

P. L. Travers

Illustrated by Mary Shepard

HARCOURT BRACE JOVANOVICH, PUBLISHERS

San Diego   New York   London

TAUG 1 1 1994

To

Elizabeth Russell Haigh
and
Anne Cordelia Crampton

Copyright ©1962 by P. L. Travers Limited

All rights reserved. No part of this publication may be reproduced or transmitted in any form or by any means, electronic or mechanical, including photocopy, recording, or any information storage and retrieval system, without permission in writing from the publisher.

Requests for permission to make copies of any part of the work should be mailed to: Permissions, Harcourt Brace Jovanovich, Publishers, Orlando, Florida 32887

Library of Congress Cataloging-in-Publication Data
Travers, P. L. (Pamela L.), 1906-
Mary Poppins from A to Z.

Reprint. Originally published: New York : Harcourt, Brace & World, 1962.
Summary: For each letter of the alphabet, there is a one-page description of a character or incident based on the other Mary Poppins books, which contains the letter in question appearing many times at the beginning of words.
[1. Alphabet.   2. Fantasy] I. Shepard, Mary,
1909-   ill. II. Title.
PZ7.T689Mas1   1985   [E]   85–16390
ISBN 0–15–252590–4

Printed in the United States of America
F G H I J K

The story of this Alphabet is about the Banks family, whose home is in Cherry-Tree Lane. It is a Delightful thoroughfare, and Everyone who lives in it knows the Five Banks children.

Jane and Michael are the two eldest. John and Barbara, the twins, come next, and the baby is Annabel.

Then there is Mrs. Brill, who cooks Good, plain, sensible meals; Ellen, the parlormaid, who suffers from hay fever; and Robertson Ay, who should look after the House and garden but who does not care for hard work.

Admiral Boom lives at the corner. His house is Imposing and built like a ship. He loves to sing songs and Joke with the children.

Next door is an elegant residence. It belongs to Kind Miss Lark, who shares it with her two dogs.

In addition to all this, Mary Poppins has come to stay at Number Seventeen. It was a great Occasion when the East Wind blew her to the Banks household, with her Parrot-headed umbrella and her carpet-bag. She has Quite altered the life of the lane, for though she is so Respectable, the Strangest things happen when she Takes charge. The children are sure she is Unlike anybody else in the world and would Very much like her to stay forever.

"I'll stay till the Wind changes," she says. "But I cannot give you the eXact date. Now, brush Your hair, tie your shoelaces, put your toys in the proper place, and do not behave like wild bears. This is a nursery, let me remind you, not a cage in the Zoo."

A is for Annabel. And here she is, out for an Airing, on Mary Poppins' Arm.

Andrew, Miss Lark's dog, is Asking for some of her Arrowroot biscuit And taking An Ample bite.

This is Against Miss Lark's Advice.

"Now, not Another crumb!" she says. "It will Affect your Appetite, And you Are having Asparagus for dinner."

Andrew is Anxious And Alarmed. Asparagus is All very well, but what he really likes is Almonds, with one or two Antelope cutlets And A slice of Apple pie.

Miss Lark takes Absolutely no notice. She is far too Agitated. "Actually, Mary Poppins," she says, "we Are looking for Robertson Ay. I want him to Assist me in Attacking the Ants in my garden."

"He's Asleep in An Armchair in the Attic," Mary Poppins Answers.

"Asleep? In the Afternoon? How Amazing!" Miss Lark is quite Astounded. She is not Aware, Apparently, that Robertson Ay, though Agreeable, Always Avoids Activity. And he falls Asleep At Any time, Anyhow, Anywhere.

B

B is for Admiral Boom, who is Mr. Banks' Best friend. He lives in a house Built like a Boat and wears a Blue coat with Brass Buttons.

His servant, Binnacle, a retired Bandit, Bakes the Bread, Borrows Butter from Mrs. Banks, and Bangs the Barometer. Today it says "Bright and Breezy," so they are Both Bringing Barbara Banks to Buy some Breadcrumbs from the Bird Woman.

"Feed the Birds!" she says Benevolently. "Only tuppence a Bag."

The Birds peck up the crumbs with their Beaks. "What a Beautiful Banquet!" they say.

And By and By, when Barbara is in Bed, the Bird Woman Beckons her Birds Beside her. They Burrow Beneath her Big Black skirts; they sit on her Bonnet; they creep into her Bulky pocket and even, Between-times, into her Boots.

"Sleep well, my Birdies!" they hear her say.

And there they stay till the Break of day.

C

C is for Cherry. Mary Poppins, with her Carpet-bag and umbrella, is strolling along the lane with the Children. The Cherry trees Cover them with shade, and the Cherries drop into their mouths.

"Chew them Carefully, all of you, in Case you Crack your teeth." The Park Keeper Clambers over the fence.

"Collect your Cherrystones!" he Cries. "There is a Container at the Corner."

"We are quite Capable of Conducting ourselves Correctly," says Mary Poppins, as she Calmly Continues on her way.

A Cuckoo Chants in a Cherry tree; a Cross-eyed Cat is Chasing a Caterpillar. The sun Courses away to the west, and the stars light Candles in the sky.

"Six o'Clock. Time to turn back!" the Chimes say Clearly.

"Caw-Caw," says the Crow. "You Can no longer roam!"

And the Curlew is Calling, "Oh, Children, Come home!"

D

D is for Dinner. Mrs. Brill, quite Distracted, Dashes in with the roast Duck and nearly Drops the Dish.

"What, no Dumplings?" Mr. Banks grumbles.

"Don't be Difficult, Dear," says Mrs. Banks. "Ellen has one of her Dreadful colds, and it is Mary Poppins' Day out."

"How Distressing! Well, Drink up, Barbara! Dry your hands, John! Your hair is a Disgrace, Michael! It's Deplorable," Mr. Banks Declares. "Whenever Mary Poppins goes out, we have a Domestic Disaster. When I say Do, you all Don't; and when I say Don't, you Do!"

"Dates for Dessert, Daddy," says Jane, who is always Diplomatic.

"How Delicious!" cries Mr. Banks. "Things are not so Dismal, after all. We shall have a Delightful Dinner."

Down the stairs Darts Mary Poppins, Dressed in her Dainty best. A Dimple Dances in her cheek and a Daisy in her hat. No one says Do or Don't to her. Nobody would Dare!

E

E is for East Wind. It is blowing Exactly as it blew when Mary Poppins arrived.

Ellen is sneezing Endlessly, but Everyone Else is Enjoying the Experience. The wind Echoes in the children's Ears and tosses the Elm leaves into their Eyes.

Even Miss Lark, Enveloped in an Embroidered curtain, has Enticed her friend, the Elderly Professor, to Enter into the fun.

"What an Exciting Escapade! I feel Equal to anything this Evening! Oh, Excuse me!" he Exclaims, as the wind blows him against Mary Poppins. "I did not mean to Embrace you, madam; I am merely Enchanted to Encounter such an Example of female Excellence."

She answers with an Elegant bow and no Embarrassment. If East winds and Elderly Professors wish to Express Enthusiasm, they are Entitled to do so. But Equally they cannot Expect to have any Effect on her.

Nor on the starlings who live under the Eaves of Number Seventeen. Quite at Ease, on the Edge of their nest, they fold their wings over their Eggs and keep the wind away.

F

F is For the Fifth of November and also the Fourth of July. These are the nights For Fireworks.

The Banks Family and their Faithful Friends are Frisking round a Fountain of Flame.

Rockets go Fizzing through the air and Fall like starry Feathers.

The children, in Flannel dressing gowns, are Flashing sparklers to and Fro.

Admiral Boom puts a match to a Flowerpot and plays a tune on his Flute.

"Follow the Fleet and Fly with me
Far away to the Foaming sea!"

The whole lane is Flooded with light.

"You could Fry a Fish in it," says the Policeman. "Send For the Fire brigade!"

"Fiddlesticks, my dear Fellow!" says Mr. Banks, quite Flabbergasted. "If anything Fearful should occur, we can just Fetch Mary Poppins."

But Mary Poppins, on the First Floor, has Forgotten the Festive occasion. With her Feet Folded on a Footstool, she is having Forty winks. Just Fancy!

G

G is for Geese. Jane and Michael, as Good as Gold, are feeding them on the Green by the lake.

Mr. Banks, whose name is George, Greets the Group as he Goes by. "What are you Giving them?" he asks.

"Grass, Gravel, Grubs, and Gumdrops!"

"Gracious!" Mr. Banks Groans. "I'm Glad I'm not a Goose!"

"They are Gallant swans in disguise," says Jane. "And Michael is really a Giant Killer, and I am Goldilocks."

"And I never Guessed it!" Mr. Banks Grins. "Did you know that I was a Grand Duke? I play the Guitar in the Gayest way and never have to pay the Grocer."

"If you Got a wish, Mary Poppins," says Michael, "what Great person would you be?"

She Gives him a Gleaming, self-satisfied Glance.

"Mary Poppins," she says.

H

H is for Herbert, the Matchman. He Huddles on the pavement, drawing Hundreds of pictures.

Today He Has made a Ham sandwich, a Hurdy-gurdy, and a bunch of Heather.

"How Handsome you look," He says Humbly, as Mary Poppins Hails Him, and He snatches up the bunch of Heather and puts it into Her Hand.

Jane and Michael can Hardly believe it.

"It isn't me; it's Her," says Herbert. "Strange things Happen when she's Here. Have a Ham sandwich if you're Hungry. It won't Hurt you; it's real."

They take a Huge bite. It is Ham, indeed.

Then the Hurdy-gurdy begins to play.

"Heave Ho, my Hearties," cries Admiral Boom, Heavily dancing the sailor's Hornpipe.

Heel and toe, Hopping like Hares, they Hurtle after Him. Oh, what a Happy Holiday!

Then, suddenly, Mary Poppins says "Home!" and everything comes to a Halt.

How Horrid to Have to Hurry away. Never mind. Perhaps there will be Honey for tea. (But T is not for Honey.)

I

I Is for In. Inside. Indoors. In a muddle. In a temper. That's where the children are today, because It Is raining outside. They are all Impatient and Irritable and can't Imagine what to do.

"Imitate me," says Mary Poppins, as she Irons her apron of Irish linen. "Get some Ink and draw an Island, with Ivy and Indians on It. Or Invent a story about an Italian who lives In an Igloo with an Ibex called Isabel. I," she adds Importantly, "am always Industrious, never Idle."

Then suddenly the weather Improves, and the Ice-Cream Man comes along the lane.

"If you behave like Intelligent children, you may put on India-rubber boots and go and Inquire the price."

Immediately their Ill-nature vanishes. How Inspired of Mary Poppins! Nothing Is Impossible now.

Ice cream! What a good Idea!

J

J is for Jane and also for John. Here they are, full of Joy, in the park's wild corner, which is like a Jungle or a Jigsaw puzzle.

"Having high Jinks?" asks the Park Keeper Jovially, shooing a Jackdaw and Jabbing at some litter.

"We're picking Jasmine and Juniper to take home to put in a Jam Jar."

"No picking of flowers in the park. Observe the rules, my Jewels, or I'll have you off to Jail in a Jiffy."

Mary Poppins Jerks her head round the *Ladies' Journal* for June.

"I'm the best Judge of that," she says Jealously. "They are simply out on a Jolly Jaunt and doing no harm to anyone. Jog along on your own Job and don't go Jeering at other people."

The Park Keeper Jumps like a Jack-in-the-box and trembles like a Jelly.

"Jiminy! What a Jolt you gave me! I didn't mean to give them the Jimjams. It was Just my Joke," he says.

K is for King. He has a private Key to the park, and when the King-
dom does not need him, he comes to fly his Kite. It is made of a Kitchen
tablecloth and trimmed with Kid and Kapok.

Today the Kite gets caught in his robes.

"Here's a pretty Kettle of fish," says the King. "I should have
worn my Kilt."

Michael Kowtows respectfully.

"Keep the string tight, your Majesty. It must not have a single
Kink. Tie it to the Knob of your crown, Kick with your feet, and run."

The King gives him a Keen glance. "What Kind advice," he
says. "You shall have a Kangaroo for a Keepsake. Are you Keeping
well, Miss Poppins? I would like to invite you all to the Kiosk for a
snack of Kippers and Kidney beans and perhaps a few nut Kernels.
But, alas, I simply haven't a Kopeck. Well, well, I must be off. There
is Kedgeree for lunch today, and the thought of it Kindles my appetite."

And away he sails, like a ship on its Keel, with his robes trailing
along the Kerb and the Kite flying behind him.

L is for Luck. Along the Lane comes the Chimney Sweep, Lugging his Load of brushes.

"Let me in, Lords and Ladies! I'll Labor to Leave your chimneys clean. And it's Lucky to shake the hand of a sweep."

Miss Lark, Leaning over her gate, Lets him Lay a Little black spot upon her Lily-white finger. Then, Lifting the Admiral's Large hand, he marks it so Lavishly with soot that it Looks Like a Leopard's paw.

The children come Leaping into his arms and Lean their cheeks on his.

"I can guess what you want, my Larrikins! Let me Label you."

He Lathers their arms and Legs with soot. "There! A black Lamb is a Lucky Lamb, all the Legends say."

He gives Mary Poppins a Languishing smile as his hand Lingers on hers. "Your eyes are Like blue Lamps, my Love, and your Lips are Lotus blossoms."

"Get along," she says Loftily. "I've no time to Loiter."

"Observe the Law," says the Park Keeper. "No Litter to be Left in the Lane!"

But the Sweep just Looks at him and Laughs. "Listen, Fred, I don't Leave Litter; I Leave Luck."

And Lightly down the Park Keeper's nose he draws a Long black Line.

"There! If you've got Luck, you Lack nothing. Learn that Lesson, Lad!"

M

M is for Michael and Mary Poppins. They are coming home from the Market with Meat and Marmalade.

"Just a Minute," says Mary Poppins. "The Mousetrap is Missing. How Mysterious!"

The Park Keeper, Mowing the lawns, picks up a Metal object. He is about to Mention it when who should March past but the Lord Mayor. He eyes the Park Keeper Moodily. "How Many times have I said, My Man, you Must Manage to be More Methodical? No Mess Must be Made in the public park. Put that Mousetrap in the Municipal litter basket."

"But, Milord, I Meant to give it—"

"Don't Mumble and Mutter," says the Lord Mayor. "Be Mindful and don't Make such a Mistake again. Ah, My dear Miss Mary Poppins! What Mild weather for the Middle of May!" And, bowing in a Majestic Manner, he Meanders on his way.

"Mine, I think," Murmurs Mary Poppins, putting out her hand for the Mousetrap.

"It was you that Mislaid it," says the Park Keeper, "and Me that has to face the Music."

"Meet Misfortune Manfully," she says with a Modest smile.

And she and Michael and the Mousetrap go home for the Midday Meal.

N

N is for Nursery. Naturally.

It may look Neglected and untidy, with Nicknacks and Ninepins scattered about. But Mary Poppins is always Neat.

The children may be Noisy and Naughty, but Mary Poppins is Never at a loss. She just says, "Now, No Nonsense, please!" And None of them Needs to be told twice.

And sometimes, in a Noble mood, she takes her Needle and hems a Napkin and Narrates the story of Noah's Ark or what happened Next to Nellie Rubina.

They Nestle against her like birds in a Nest.

Nobody Notices Night is Near.

Their heads are Nodding on their Necks. Nid-Nod, Nid-Nod.

The Nightingale sings a Note in the park.

The New moon rises, but No one sees.

Within the Nursery Nothing stirs.

"Number seventeen," say the Neighbors, "is Nice and quiet tonight."

O is for Once-upon-a-time. And here's an Original story.

One day in October, the children were playing Out in the lane when the Old lady Opposite the gate Offered to sell them her balloons.

"Only One penny! Oblige me, do!"

So, they seized the Opportunity, and then an Odd thing Occurred. The balloons flew up Over the park, pulling the children with them.

"Do they Often do this?" cried Jane and Michael.

"Occasionally," the balloon woman answered. "Oh, dear, I Omitted to tie the strings! Here I am, blowing away On my Own!"

And there she went, sailing up Over the Oak trees, Opening her arms to the sky, as though she were Off to Orion.

"Observe the rules!" the Park Keeper shouted. "You Ought to know better. It's Outrageous!"

But the Other Onlookers Only smiled. "Now, don't Oppose them Or be Officious. It's a very Orderly Occupation. That is Our Opinion!"

P

P is for Park. Along the Path the Policeman Paces, a Pillar of the law.

"Please Put your Paper in the Proper basket," the Park Keeper Pleads.

Down the Parade comes a little Procession. Mary Poppins, carrying her Parrot-headed umbrella, is Pushing the Perambulator. And beside her, Playing with the children, are a Polar bear and a Penguin.

"Preserve the law!" the Policeman shouts. "Wild beasts not Permitted in Public Places."

The Park Keeper's face turns as Pale as Putty. "Polar bears in the Park!" he Pants. "I must Point it out to the Prime Minister."

"Pray don't!" Protests the Prime Minister, who is Passing through the Park. "I have already Perceived the Problem. May I Provide Protection, Miss Poppins? I have a Pistol in my Pocket."

"Thank you," she replies Primly. "I can Preserve myself. We are having a Purely Private Party. These are my Personal friends."

"In that case, madam, I beg your Pardon."

And the Prime Minister Plods on, Pondering on Politics and feeling quite at Peace. He knows that when Mary Poppins makes a Plan, it will always Prove to be Pleasant, Practical, and Prudent—in fact, Pretty nearly Perfect.

Q is for Question.

The Queen asks, "Why are Quinces yellow? And do they Quench the thirst? Does a hen," she Queries, "think it Quaint when ducklings say Quack-Quack?" And she goes on asking, asking till the King gives her a Quelling look and tells her not to Quibble.

And what about you? Can *you* answer Questions? Did you know, for instance, that Quantities of Quill pens require a Quart of ink, not to mention a Quire of paper?

Have you heard that Quails Quaff water once a Quarter and always have Quadruplets?

Or that Quadrupeds, before Quitting a Quest, will dance the Quadrille without a Qualm, all standing in Queues?

"Isn't it Queer that we Quarrel one day and the next we're Quite friendly?" say Jane and Michael Querulously.

"Quiet, please," says Mary Poppins, "and Quickly into bed, spitspot."

"Are our Quilts of good Quality, Mary Poppins? Why does a jelly Quiver and Quake?"

"A dose of Quinine," she says Quizzically, "for the one who asks the next Question!"

R

R is for Robertson Ay.

Today he is Responsible for a Really awful Rumpus. He has Rubbed Mr. Banks' hat with an oily Rag instead of a Rabbit's tail.

"He's a broken Reed, a Rattlebrain. I'll be glad to be Rid of the Rogue!" Mr. Banks Rages up and down. "The Rascal, the Reptile, the Reprobate!"

"He didn't Realize," say the children. "He is not Robust, and he needs to Rest."

"Rubbish!" Mr. Banks Retorts. "He is Required to Run errands and Render assistance, Rake the ashes, Repair the Railings, Rout the Rats— and what does he do? Reposes in a Rocking chair, wholly Regardless of the fact that I'm Rapidly losing my Reason. And on top of that, he Ruins my hat! I shall look Ridiculous!"

"Oh, let him Remain, Daddy! Don't Refuse!"

"Well, only if he Reforms, Remember!"

Full of Rapture and Relief, they Rush away to Robertson Ay with the Reassuring news.

But Robertson Ay is as Right as Rain. Nothing Ruffles him.

Rosy with sleep, wrapped in Mr. Banks' traveling Rug, he Reclines against the garden Roller, taking his Regular morning Rest.

S is for Snow. Today the lane wears a Shawl of Silver. Everyone Slides and Skates and Slithers.

The Snowman has two Stones for eyes, and Binnacle, the Admiral's Servant, has lent him his old Sou'wester.

"Save me, Someone!" Shrieks Miss Lark, Skidding across the Scene.

Andrew, in his Sealskin jacket, Seizes her Skirt and Steadies her.

"No Skidding allowed!" Shouts the Park Keeper, very Superior, all day long.

But at night, when all is Still and Silent, he Steals through the Solitary park, Singing a Secret Song. Over the flower beds he Spreads the Snow, Stroking it very Softly and Slowly, as though he were Smoothing the Sheets of a bed.

"Sh!" he whispers. "Let nobody Stir. Sleep till the Spring when the Sap rises."

For the Seeds, you See, are his children. They will Slumber through the dark Season, but the first Sign of Spring will Set them moving. Their new Small Spikes, So green and Shiny, will Shoot up through the Sod.

And how the Park Keeper's eyes will Sparkle!

"For once," he will Say, "the rules are observed! The Sunflower turns to the Sun again, and the Swallows are back from the South!"

T

T is for Topsy-Turvy.

It is Tuesday. Mr. Banks Tears Through The house like a Tempest.

"Why is my Tobacco Tin Topped-up with Toffee? Who Tied my Tartan Tie round The Toast?"

No one can Tell him.

Nothing is Turning out right This morning. Tapioca in The Teapot and The Teapot out on The Terrace. Trousers in The soup Tureen. Tomatoes Tasting of Tar.

"Tush, it's a Trifle," says Mary Poppins. "Never Trouble Trouble! If Today is a Tiny bit Topsy-Turvy, we must Treat The whole Thing Tactfully and Turn Topsy-Turvy, Too."

So, Taking up her Tulip-Trimmed hat, she Twirls Through The air like a spinning Top and lands Triumphantly on her head, Tidy and Totally Tranquil.

"Take your Time. Don't Teeter or Totter. Try To do as you are Told!"

"What a sensible Trick," the children say, as They Tumble Through The room Together and land on The Turkey carpet. "It is True what you Taught us, Mary Poppins. Everything seems Transformed."

"To Turn with The Tide," says Mary Poppins, "is To Take a Turn for The better. May I Tempt you with a Tangerine and a Topsy-Turvy Tart?"

U

U is for Unicorn. This animal is very Unusual and rarely to be found. Try your Utmost, hunt through all the Universe, and you still may not Unearth him.

But don't be Upset. If you have Untroubled eyes, you will see what the children see. Under Mary Poppins' Umbrella, white as the Upper part of a mushroom, with a single horn Upon his brow, reclines a Unicorn!

The Policeman, in his new blue Uniform, stares Uneasily.

"What are those Urchins at?" he wonders. "All so United, gaping at nothing? Something Urgent is Up, but what?"

An Upright figure, Unafraid, handsome rather than Ugly, he turns to Mary Poppins.

"Don't think me Ultra fussy, Miss, but is anything Undesirable going on Unbeknownst?"

She gives him an Uppish look and sniffs. "Nothing Unseemly ever happens when I'm around," she assures him.

He passes on Unconvinced. "I'm not Used to Riddles," he tells himself. "But I'm not an Utter idiot. I'll Unravel it Ultimately, I'm sure."

But this, I think, is most Unlikely.

Unicorns are shy creatures.

They will Undertake to Unveil themselves only Under parrot-headed Umbrellas to those who are Untouched by doubt and who can Understand.

V

V is for Valentine's Day. The children are Visiting Mrs. Corry's sweet shop to ask her to be their Valentine. She is Visibly pleased.

"Now, what do you Vote for? Vanilla sticks?" she asks.

And she Vigorously breaks off two of her fingers and gives them to the children.

"Don't look so Vacant; they'll grow again! And in many Varieties. Violet candy is now in Vogue. And Queen Victoria, I Vividly recall, had a Violent fondness for Vinegar mints."

"How old you must be!" say Jane and Michael.

"Venerable is the word, my dears. I remember Henry V saying,

'Your Vegetable fudge with honey
Is splendid Value for the money.'

"He spoke in Verse and, though Vague, was not Vulgar. What, are you going? How Vexatious. Well, take a piece of Verbena toffee. Never put Vaseline on your Vests. If a Villain pursues you, wear a Veil. Bon Voyage!" she said, and Vanished.

"How Very odd! We were just on the Verge of thanking her. Mary Poppins," the children ask, "does this always happen on Valentine's Day?"

"It all depends on the point of View," is Mary Poppins' Verdict.

W is for Willoughby. He is Miss Lark's other dog, Who is half an airedale and half a retriever and the Worst half of both.

Andrew is a Winsome dog and Welcome everywhere. But no one seems to Want Willoughby.

Miss Lark is Worn out With his Wild Ways.

"He is Willfully Wallowing in Wickedness. I must take a cup of Weak tea!" she Whispers. "Oh, Why Won't you try to be Well-bred, Willoughby? Can't you Wag your tail Without Whacking the Window? Must you Wipe your paws on the White Woodwork?"

But Willoughby only replies With a Wink and Whisks off after a Wasp.

"He's a Werewolf!" says the Park Keeper, as Willoughby Whizzes past him. "Observe the rules or I'll get a Whip. No Washing your Whiskers in the lake!"

"Woof!" says Willoughby, Whirling the Water off his back and Wetting the Park Keeper's Waistcoat.

Then he Worries a Woodpecker out of its Wits, Worms his Way under the park Wall, and Waltzes home, Wondering Whether there Will be chicken for dinner. If so, he Wants the Wishbone.

Even When he is asleep, Weary and Warm in his Wicker basket, Willoughby still is on the Warpath, chasing Weasels through his dreams and Walruses and Whales.

X

X is for no special word unless you can count Xylophone.

But nevertheless, it is very important, for what do you put at the end of a letter? X for a kiss, of course.

And the one who gets it knows you love him and feels eXtremely happy.

Here in the picture is Mr. Banks, and because he is in an eXpansive mood, he is X-ing Mrs. Banks.

The Policeman is shyly X-ing Ellen.

The Prime Minister is asking if he may X Miss Lark's hand.

And the children are X-ing Andrew and Willoughby.

But the poor Park Keeper is all alone.

Has he been forgotten, I wonder?

Why don't *you* give him an X?

Y is for Year. And the Year changes all.

In spring the cherry trees were green. They were white with flowers in summertime, red in autumn with their Yield of fruit, and now they are black and bare.

The goslings on the lake, once Yellow as the Yolks of eggs, have gray feathers now. The birds that Yearned over their Young have flown from the Yew tree Yonder. The children's shoes, Yet too large in January, are now too small in December.

There they all are, down in the lane, Yelling and dancing to keep warm and wishing for Yakskin coats.

Andrew is Yapping at their heels, and Willoughby, like a Yahoo, is Yawning in everyone's face.

"The Year is going," says Mary Poppins.

"Where does it go?" the children ask.

And a deep familiar voice answers:

> "The Year goes where our dreams all go,
>   East of the sun and west of the moon,
>   Where tomorrow is always behind us
>   And Yesterday comes too soon.
>   So Yank up the anchor and sail away
>   On the Yacht of Yours truly, Admiral Boom.

"Just one of my Yarns!" he says. "Well, messmates, looking forward to Yule? That's what Christmas was called when I was a bit of a Youngster."

What a happy thought! Trimming the tree, hanging the stockings, and unpacking them in the morning. Christmas or Yule, what does it matter?

"Yes!" says everyone.

𝒵

Z is for Zodiac. That means the ring of stars and planets that circles the earth at night.

This evening it is specially bright, for it is New Year's Eve.

All the neighbors are full of song and Zest as they greet each other in the lane.

"Walk straight, Willoughby," says Miss Lark. "Kindly do not Zigzag." And she beats time Zealously to the sound of the Admiral's Zither.

"Oh, I'm off to the Zone of the Zephyrs."

Mr. Banks takes up the song with Zeal, and everyone joins in. Even the animals in the Zoo, especially the Zebras and Zebus, are shouting it merrily.

"Oh, I'm off to the Zone of the Zephyrs
    In New Zealand and Zanzibar.
I have Zipped up my slippers,
I'm skipping with trippers
    And Zulus in Zanzibar!"

"No Zulus to be left in the lane!" cries the Park Keeper wildly.

"What a Zany you are," says Mr. Banks. "The number of Zulus here is Zero."

At that moment the clock strikes twelve. Bells ring out from all the steeples, echoing up to the sky's Zenith to tell the lovely news.

"The New Year's born!" cries everyone. "Let us welcome it!"

Mary Poppins puts her arms round the children as they sing the Admiral's song.

"A happy New Year, Jane and Michael!" she says. "Now, say good night to each and all. Zip up your slippers, no more skipping with trippers. From A to Z the alphabet's read. And now we must all go to bed."

All night long the Zodiac shines, warming the newborn Year. There is no other light in the lane, eXcept the one in the top Window of the Very smallest house. Up there, the faithful night-light Twinkles, Sending its protecting Rays over the Quiet nursery. The Parrot-headed umbrella is hanging On its accustomed hook. The carpet-bag is in the cupboard. Everything is Neat and tidy.

Mary Poppins, as she undresses, Looks along the line of beds. Michael has Kicked a blanket away. John has flung off his eiderdown. She tucks them both In comfortably and Hushes Annabel in her cot.

Then she Goes across to Jane's bed to Fill the empty glass with water and picks up Barbara's Elephant, which has fallen to the floor.

Her Day's work is over now. One more glance at the sleeping children, then she winds the Clock on the mantelpiece and daintily steps into Bed.

For a moment she ponders the Alphabet. "It embraces everything," she thinks. "All that is or was or will be lies between A and Z."

Then she yawns. Huh-huh. Huh-huh.

Without thinking another thought, she pulls the covers over her shoulders. And in something less than half a second, Mary Poppins, too, is Asleep.

NILES PUBLIC LIBRARY